THE SEA-THING CHILD

For Leon Redler

To the above 1972 dedication I have pleasure in
adding sea-thing greetings to my newest grandchild,
Paul, born April 22, 1998

R.H.

For Sarah Franklyn and Francis Joyce

P.B.

Text copyright © 1972, 1999 by Russell Hoban
Illustrations copyright © 1999 by Patrick Benson

Second U.S. edition 1999

Library of Congress Cataloging-in-Publication Data

Hoban, Russell.
The sea-thing child / Russell Hoban ; illustrated by Patrick Benson.—2nd U.S. ed.
p.   cm.
Summary: Washed up on the beach during a storm, the sea-thing child
clings fearfully to the shore until he discovers his true destiny.
ISBN 0-7636-0847-5
[1. Seashore—Fiction. 2. Birds—Fiction.] I. Benson, Patrick, ill. II. Title.
PZ7.H637Se   1999
[Fic]—dc21   98-53936

2 4 6 8 10 9 7 5 3 1

Printed in Italy

This book was typeset in Giovanni Book.
The illustrations were done in pen and ink, and watercolor.

Candlewick Press
2067 Massachusetts Avenue
Cambridge, Massachusetts 02140

THE SEA-THING CHILD

Russell Hoban

ILLUSTRATED BY

Patrick Benson

CANDLEWICK PRESS
CAMBRIDGE, MASSACHUSETTS

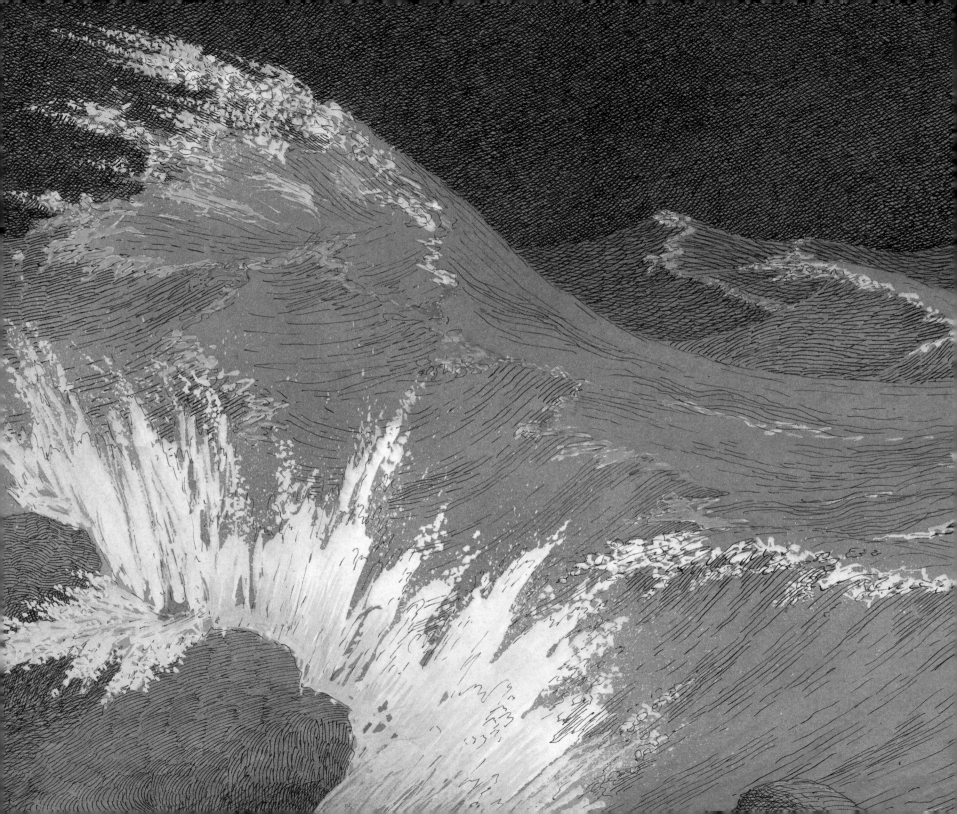

The wind was howling, the sea was wild, and the night was black when the storm flung the sea-thing child up on the beach. In the morning the sky was fresh and clean, the beach was littered with seaweed, and there he lay — a little black heap of scales and feathers, all alone.

All alone he was, and behind him the ocean roared and shook its fist. He lay there, howling not very loud, "Ow, ow, ow! Ai-ee!" while the foam washed over him and went hissing away again. He was too little to swim very well and he hadn't learned to fly yet. He was nothing but a little draggled heap of fright.

After a while he crawled up among the big old seaweed-bearded rocks by a tide pool, and he went to sleep there, cheeping softly to himself.

When he woke up, he ate some seaweed and some mussels and he felt stronger. He listened to the pebbles clicking in the tide-wash as the tide came in. Then he gathered up some round stones and some broken bits of bottles, cups, and saucers that the sea and sand had smoothed to lumps of sea glass and sea china.

He built a sea-stone igloo all around himself with no door and no window. Then he sat inside it, breathing hard and making faces.

After a while he heard a thin and whispery voice yelling, "Oh, if only I had a bow, what music I could play!" The voice sounded as if it came from something smaller than the sea-thing child, so he peeped through a space between the stones of his igloo.

He saw a fiddler crab waving his fiddle and shouting, "Oh, oh, oh! If only I had a bow, what music I could play! Walruses and great green turtles from the trackless deep would gather to the sound of my fiddling, yes."

The sea-thing child pushed some stones off the top of his igloo and stuck his head out. "Why don't you have a bow?"

"What a brutal question!" said the crab, and he began to cry. The sea-thing child began to cry too. When they had finished crying, the sea-thing child said, "But why *don't* you have a bow?"

"If fiddler crabs had bows," said the crab, "the noise of their fiddling would be deafening, and nobody could hear the long, long magic curve of silence arching underneath the day's long sky. As far as I can see, you are a nobody and you come out of nowhere. And you want to change everything."

"But you were the one who was complaining," said the sea-thing child. "I wasn't."

"Oh ho," said the crab. His eye-stalks stood straight up. "I was *not* complaining, and everything was all right until you showed up."

"If you say so," said the sea-thing child. He pulled his head back into his sea-stone igloo, put the stones back on top, and sat in the dark and made faces.

After a while the crab said, "Are you there?"

"Yes," said the sea-thing child.

"Do you still think I should have a bow?" said the crab.

"I don't want to make trouble," said the sea-thing child.

"I want you to be frank with me," said the crab.

The sea-thing child stuck his head out of his igloo. "How many fiddler crabs are there around here?" he said.

"I am the only one," said the crab. "This is a one-fiddler-crab beach."

"In that case," said the sea-thing child, "I think the sound of your fiddle would make one hear even better the long, long magic curve of silence."

"Thank you," said the crab. And he began to cry.

"Why are you crying now?" said the sea-thing child.

"I don't want to talk about it," said the crab, sniffling and sobbing. "Let us put this matter off to another time and go strolling in the foam."

The sea-thing child looked out at the white foam, the sparkling surf, the green waves, and the deep and dark blue line of ocean where it met the sky. Then he pulled his head in and put the stones back on top of his sea-stone igloo.

"I don't want to go strolling in the foam," he said.

"All right," said the crab. "But will you come out and play?"

"What do you want to play?" said the sea-thing child.

"Stones?" said the crab.

"Yes," said the sea-thing child. He took off the top of his igloo and came out. He and the crab played stones all afternoon, and while they played they sang:

Perfectly round is seldom found,

But egg shapes are abounding.

The sea-thing child was restless in the night, and he left his igloo and went for a walk on the beach all alone, not very close to the edge of the water where the white foam gleamed in the dark. He walked to where a river ran down to the sea, and there he heard an eel singing as it came down the river:

> *Fresh to salt,*
>> *Salt to deep.*
>> *Need must find —*
>> *Finding knows*
>> *Water goes*
>>> *Fresh to salt,*
>> *Salt to deep,*
>>> *Deep to finding.*

"Where are you going?" said the sea-thing child.

"Far and deep," said the eel. "Far and deep."

The sea-thing child looked at the ocean that was black in the night. "How will you find your way?" he said.

"Finding knows," said the eel, dark in the starshine on the river. "The finding is in me, and the finding finds the way."

"Aren't you afraid?" said the sea-thing child.

"Of what?" said the eel, slipping through the water, tasting in his mouth the sea brine and the salt night.

"Of the deepness and the darkness and the farness of the sea," said the sea-thing child.

When the eel answered, he was out beyond the foam, and his voice was almost lost in the slap and gurgle of the waves. "*Born* for the sea!" he called, and headed for the deeps.

The next day the sea-thing child fussed with his igloo all morning, and when the fiddler crab came to visit him, he said that he did not want to play stones again.

"Perhaps today is a good day for strolling in the foam?" said the crab.

"Why don't you make a bow for your fiddle," said the sea-thing child, "and then you can play beautiful music while we stroll in the foam. And perhaps the walruses and green turtles will come strolling in the foam with us."

When the crab heard that, he scuttled into his hole and cried all afternoon.

That night the sea-thing child took his igloo apart and scattered his sea stones and sea glass and sea china all over the beach. He went down to the edge of the foam that gleamed in the dark and he smelled the salt air and listened to the surf. He waded in and felt the dark water flow past his tail. He went deeper, and it wet the scales on his belly. The water was warm, but he knew that farther out he would feel the cold coming up from the deeps. A little wave broke over his head and ran past, then the bottom tried to slide away from under his feet and pull him out to deep water with it. "Ai-ee!" said the sea-thing child.

He came out of the water and ran up to the big old seaweed-bearded rocks. He built his igloo all around him again with no door and no window, and he went to sleep, cheeping in the dark.

The fiddler crab and the sea-thing child had very little to say to each other for a while. The sea-thing child kept making igloos and taking them apart, and as time passed he had to make them bigger and bigger because he was growing fast.

One day an albatross landed on the beach, pulled a little stubby pipe out, and sat down to have a smoke. The fiddler crab hid among the rocks but the sea-thing child came over to talk to the albatross.

"Ahoy," said the albatross. "Nice beach you've got here. Good landing strip. Good fishing. Good rocks. Nice place." He puffed big clouds of smoke from his little black pipe and stared out to sea with fearless eyes. "You don't happen to play the fiddle or anything like that, do you? I like a bit of music and fun when I'm ashore."

"No," said the sea-thing child. "But I have a friend who has a fiddle."

"No bow," said the fiddler crab from his hiding place in the rocks.

"Oh, well," said the albatross. "I'll just sit awhile and enjoy the view then. Fine day. See for miles. Lovely wind. Good flying. Made a fine passage today. Miles and miles and miles. But of course you know how it is as well as I do, you being a sea-thing."

"Yes," said the sea-thing child. "I'm a sea-thing."

"Fly and swim, just like me," said the albatross. "But you can go *under*, too. You can do the deep swimming. What have you seen down in the deeps?"

"I've never seen anything," said the sea-thing child, "except the big storm that blew me out of my nest and washed me up here."

"Don't tell me you've been on the beach all this time," said the albatross.

"Yes, I have," said the sea-thing child.

"How come?" said the albatross.

"Well, the storm, you know," said the sea-thing child, "and the wind and the waves and the dark, and the ocean being so big and me so small."

"Small!" said the albatross. "What *isn't* small compared to the ocean! The blue whale's the biggest thing that swims, and that's small in the *ocean*. If the ocean weren't big it wouldn't be the ocean. The whale is whale-size, I'm albatross-size, and you're sea-thing-size. What more do you want?" He stood up and brushed the sand off his bottom.

"You're never afraid?" said the sea-thing child. "Not afraid of getting lost in the middle of the ocean? Not afraid of the storms and the dark and the wind howling all around you?"

"There's no such thing as an afraid albatross," said the albatross. "The ocean wouldn't be the ocean without storms, and the ocean is where I live. How can you get lost when you're where you live? I was born on a rock in the middle of the ocean, and Wandering is my name." He knocked the ash from his pipe and turned into the wind. "Clear the runway," he said. "I'm taking off." He started his run, flapped his wings hard, and went up into the air.

The sea-thing child watched the albatross out of sight. Then he went back to one of the big old seaweed-bearded rocks and sat on it all afternoon, looking out to sea until the sky grew dark.

The sea-thing child stopped building igloos but sometimes he made little heaps of stones and sea glass and sea china and drew a circle in the sand around them and sat inside the circle.

"Do you make a break in the circle when you want to come out or do you just step over it?" said the crab.

"I have to make a break in the circle, of course," said the sea-thing child, "but that's much less bother than moving stones and much easier to close up again."

"Yes," said the crab. "That's very sensible. It's a fine day. Perhaps we might take a walk among the rocks?"

"Why don't we stroll in the foam?" said the sea-thing child.

"In the foam," said the crab. "Right in it, you mean, where it's wet?"

"Yes," said the sea-thing child. He rubbed out just enough of the circle so that he could walk through the space. Then he closed it up again, and they went strolling in the foam, singing the song the sea sang:

Breathing and sighing, far and deep —

Hissing and foaming, never sleep.

At night the sea-thing child felt more and more restless. He looked at the stars, and when he closed his eyes, he went on seeing the stars in his mind. He could not sleep unless he was facing a particular star that burned and flickered over the sea, and when he slept he dreamed of wind rushing past him. He dreamed of the ocean too, black and heaving in the night, sometimes under him, sometimes over him. He would run along the beach in the dark, cheeping to himself, then he would come back to his circle. And every night before he went to sleep he drew a second circle around the first one.

One day when the sea-thing child woke up, the sky was gray, the sea was rough and huge, the air hummed. The sea-thing child stayed inside his double circle all day, staring at the ocean.

After a while the crab came and stood outside the double circle with his eye-stalks turned away from the sea-thing child. "You never want to play stones anymore," he said. "You never want to stroll in the foam. You are tired of listening to my lies."

"What lies?" said the sea-thing child.

"My lies about what I could do if I had a bow," said the crab.

"But you don't have a bow," said the sea-thing child.

"With a bit of bone and seaweed I could make one," said the crab, "but what if I have no music in me?"

"Need must find," said the sea-thing child.

"Find what?" said the crab.

"Whatever there is," said the sea-thing child.

"All right," said the crab. "I'll *make* the bow. Will you stay then, and not go away?"

"I never said I was going away," said the sea-thing child.

"At night I hear you running in the dark," said the crab. "Sometimes I see you looking at the stars and I hear something in the wind."

"What do you hear in the wind?" said the sea-thing child.

"Whatever there is," said the crab.

That night the sea-thing child heard the air humming. He looked up at the sky for the star that he always looked at but it was blotted out. He could not see the star with his eyes, but in the dark of his mind he saw it burning and flickering over the sea. The humming of the air grew louder, and the sea-thing child stepped out of his double circle and faced into the wind. The ocean was high and wild, and the sky and the sea roared together, heaving in the dark.

The sea-thing child spread his wings to keep from falling down and the wind blew him backwards. He moved forward against the wind, then he began to run, faster and faster. The beach slipped away from under him, he laughed and flapped his wings and left the ground behind.

When the crab heard the beating of wings he came out of his hole and looked up. "Whatever there is?" he shouted.

"Whatever there is!" called the sea-thing child. He swooped down through the dark, dived through the wild waves into the blackness below, rose up out of the foam, soared into the night and away into the storm over the ocean he was born in.

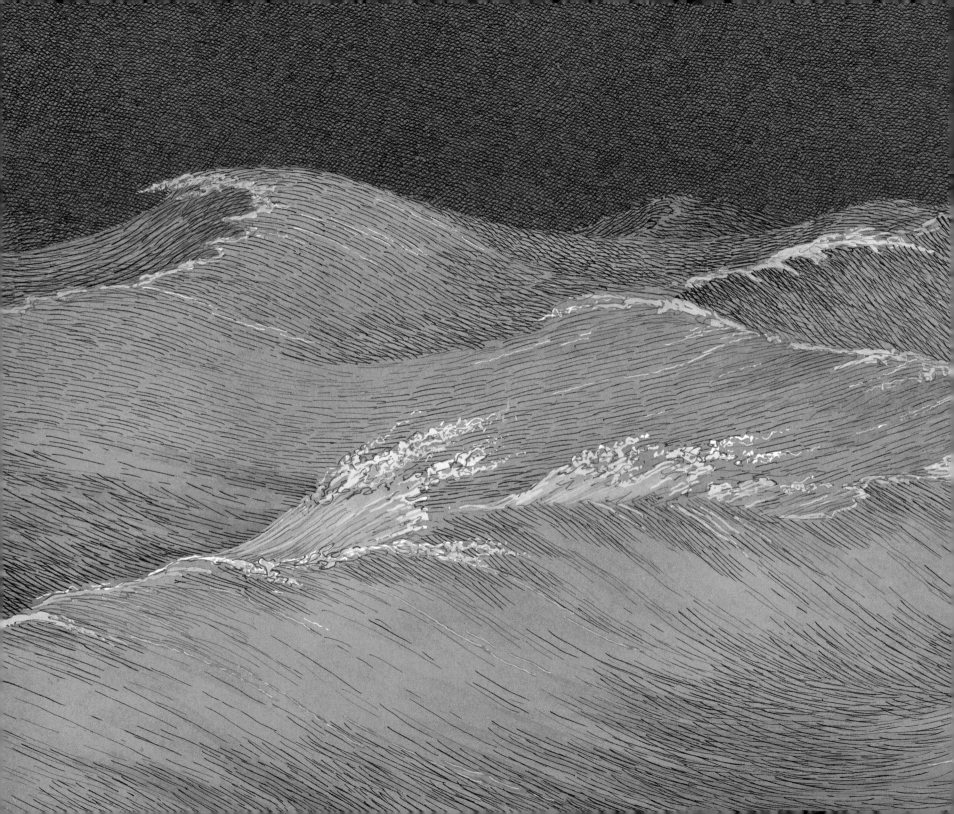